NORTH
AMERICA

CENTRAL
AMERICA

Galápagos
Islands

Ecuador

SOUTH
AMERICA

With much love to
Philip
and
to all the splendid
Galápagos
guides
and
every
blue-footed booby
besides.

Special thanks to Susan Guevara
for sharing her first-class photographs.

The Sierra Club, founded in 1892 by John Muir, has devoted itself to the study and protection of the earth's scenic and ecological resources — mountains, wetlands, woodlands, wild shores and rivers, deserts and plains. The publishing program of the Sierra Club offers books to the public as a nonprofit educational service in the hope that they may enlarge the public's understanding of the Club's basic concerns. The point of view expressed in each book, however, does not necessarily represent that of the Club. The Sierra Club has some sixty chapters in the United States and Canada. For information about how you may participate in its programs to preserve wilderness and the quality of life, please address inquiries to Sierra Club, 85 Second Street, San Francisco, CA 94105, or visit our website at http://www.sierraclub.org.

First Edition

Published by Sierra Club Books for Children
85 Second Street, San Francisco, California 94105
www.sierraclub.org/books

Published in conjunction with Gibbs Smith, Publisher
P.O. Box 667, Layton, Utah 84041
www.gibbs-smith.com

SIERRA CLUB, SIERRA CLUB BOOKS, and the Sierra Club design logos are registered trademarks of the Sierra Club.

Library of Congress Cataloging-in-Publication Data

Heller, Ruth
    "Galápagos" means "tortoises" / written and illustrated by Ruth Heller. — 1st ed.
        p. cm.
    Summary: Rhyming text and illustrations present the characteristics and behavior of animals found on the Galápagos Islands, including the giant tortoises, blue-footed boobies, and land iguanas.
    ISBN 0-87156-917-5 (alk. paper)
    1. Zoology — Galápagos Islands Juvenile literature. [1. Zoology — Galápagos Islands.] I. Title.
QL345.G2H45 2000
591.9866'5 — dc21   99-28983

Printed in Hong Kong
10 9 8 7 6 5 4 3 2 1

"GALÁPAGOS"
Means "Tortoises"

Written and illustrated by

Ruth Heller

Sierra Club Books for Children

San Francisco

These islands of enchantment
are an archipelago
formed by the eruption
and the torrid lava flow
of furious volcanos
ten million years ago.

Now
tortoises, iguanas, and boobies by the score,
and animals you may have never seen before,
live upon these islands
six hundred miles
from shore.

These
islands called
Galápagos
belong
to Ecuador.

3

Giant Tortoises

These Galápagos giants are all legendary.
From island to island,
their shapes seem to vary.
Attached to their bones, on their backs
are their homes —
shells that are shaped like saddles or domes.

Those with a dome
are usually found
grazing on grasses
close to the ground.

4

Others can dine
in rather high places
because
of their
saddle-shaped
carapaces.

5

Water and mud
are
their chosen domain.
They wallow in puddles
made by the rain.

6

They loudly expel a conspicuous hiss
whenever they feel that something's amiss.
They're sluggish and heavy
and usually slow
unless they have somewhere
important to go.

Blue-footed Boobies

They prance
and dance
and retreat
and advance.
They spread
their wings
as
they
romance.

They
exchange
small gifts
like
feathers and twigs
as
they show off
their feet
and
dance their
jigs.

And it is true their feet are blue . . .

8

. . . But they are not just . . .   . . . pretty feet . . .

9

. . . They generate warmth and radiate heat.

Then
three eggs
the female lays.
And with those feet
for forty days,
both parents help to incubate.
They equally participate.

They fly through the air
with the greatest of ease
and plunge right down
into shallow seas.
Both parents fish.
They fish a lot
and feed their chicks
with what they've caught.

A booby chick
soon grows white fluff
and looks just like
a powder puff.

Red-footed Boobies

In a bush or a tree
near the beach by the sea,
the red-footed boobies nest.

They're rather small as boobies go,
their feathers brown or white as snow.

Their feet are webbed. They nest in trees —
unusual for birds like these.

Their legs are short, and on the ground,
they waddle as they walk around.

But when they fly far out to sea,
they skim the waves so gracefully,
searching for their favorite dishes —
tentacled squid and flying fishes.

With one little booby
each couple is blessed
because only one egg
is laid in each nest.

Masked Boobies

They're the largest of the boobies
that we have so far seen.
They're bluish black around the eyes
and look as though they're in disguise.

Their feathers glisten whitely.
Their wings are fringed with black.
The males all whistle weakly.
The females loudly quack.

They're just a bit too hefty
to become airborne with ease,
so some live high upon a cliff
and take off in the breeze.

Two eggs are laid five days apart,
but just one chick survives.
The older and the larger sees
that it's the one that thrives.

Land Iguanas

Land iguanas,
brown and gold,
are in the mornings
very cold.
In the sun they bask a lot
and so by noon
are much too hot
and have to find
a shady spot.

They quench their thirst
from puddles of rain
and liquids that
their foods contain.

They never hesitate to feed
upon a passing centipede,
and
to this spiny menu add
cactus flower, fruit, and pad.

Their throats are strong and tough enough
to swallow all this prickly stuff.

Marine Iguanas

These iguanas just feed
on salty seaweed.
They eat nothing else —
that is all that they need.

They stay in the water so long
they're like ice,
so they find it essential
and also quite nice
to bask in the sun
until they get hot . . .
if they're lucky enough to find a good spot
on the volcanic rock
where all of them flock.

They're full of salt. They're caked in white.
They snort and sneeze.
They look a fright.
Not . . .

. . . a very pretty sight!
  They are usually black with a fringy white back. But . . .

. . . when
they play the mating game
and do not want to look the same,
they turn to green and red
instead.

They have serrated teeth
and
short, pudgy faces
so they can reach seaweed
in difficult places.

Half of their length is their tail.
They can grow to five feet
if they're male.

They can dive from the shore
to the cold ocean floor
and stay for an hour, but not any more.
In the dark, chilly waters
they like to stay down,
eating red and green algae
but never the brown.

The smaller iguanas
are quite satisfied
to nibble and chew from the shore
at low tide.

Sally Lightfoot Crabs

They forage for algae and scavenge for meat
and crawl right over the heads and the feet
of their neighbors, who don't seem to care
that they're there,
on the black lava rock
that the two of them share.

They make very good meals
for herons and eels.

Some claim that the name of these little red flames
that dart back and forth is exactly the same
as a dancer from Haiti a sailor once knew,
who moved when she danced
the same way that
they do.

Sea Lions

With a massive, thick neck
and a bump on his brow,
the male is a bull.

24

The female's a cow.

The female is svelte
and graceful and sleek,
with a trimmer and slimmer and
smaller physique.

25

One bull and
some cows,
maybe twenty or more,
form a group called a
"harem"
right there on the shore.

Their offspring are born,
one pup every year,
on the land, in the sand, or on rocks
that are near.

They're nosey and noisy.
They frolic and loll.
They toss small iguanas
around like a ball.

On sardines and squid
and urchins they dine,
then back to the beach
up and down the
coastline . . .

27

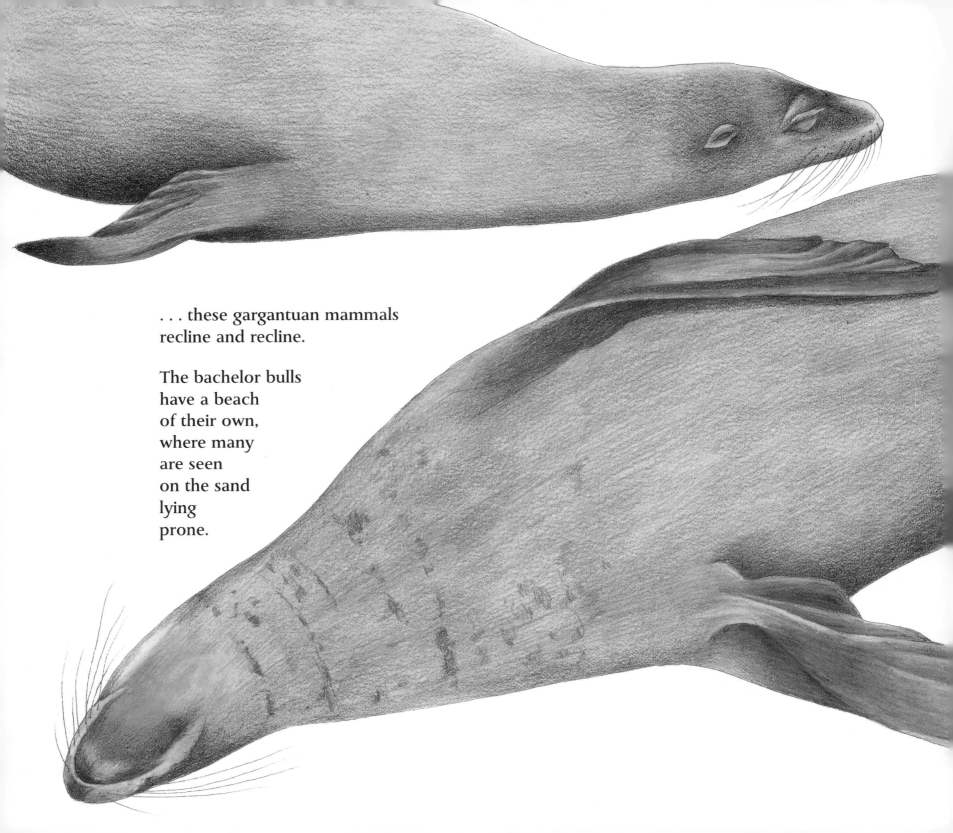

. . . these gargantuan mammals
recline and recline.

The bachelor bulls
have a beach
of their own,
where many
are seen
on the sand
lying
prone.

The bull
with his harem,
protecting his pack,
patrols
back and forth
and patrols
forth and back.

He's hostile
toward rivals.
Look out
when they
clash!

They'll fight
and they'll bite
and they'll bark
and
they'll splash.

29

Flightless Cormorants

Their necks are sinewy and long.
Their feet are webbed and very strong.
But something is completely wrong.
Those tattered wings just don't belong.

These birds no longer fly.
They never even try.
Now they leap into the deep
for eels and fish and octopi,
and
when they're through, they come ashore
and spread their wings to dry.

They go courting in the water,
swimming side by side,
flapping wings and pointing beaks
and gurgling in the tide.

The female is the architect
and builder of the nest.
The male supplies the flotsam.
The female does the rest.

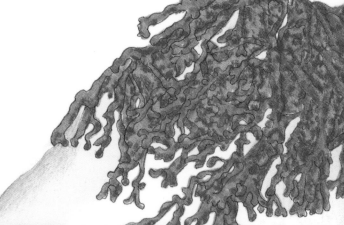

Great Frigate Birds

Frigate birds are great, all right.
They're very graceful when in flight.
They flap their wings just now and then,
and fly for miles . . . then flap again.
And they will always, always try
to keep their greenish feathers dry.
Because they are not waterproof,
getting wet's a fatal goof.
They never, ever settle down
upon the sea, or they will drown.

Frigate birds are thieves —
they steal!
From other birds they snatch a meal.

To attract an affectionate, frigate mate,
the males need merely to inflate.
The sacs at their throats that are red and small
can swell to the size of a basketball.

Together they build or steal a nest
that is floppy and sloppy
and rough at best,
where a single egg is laid, and so
if it doesn't fall out,
one chick will grow.

33

Greater Flamingos

They feed with their heads
upside down by their feet
as they gracefully wade
in the ooze.

The pinkish brine shrimp
in the salty lagoon
give them
their delicate hues.

Cleverly hidden
inside of each beak
is a filter that strains
all the food that they seek.

A spectacular sight
in the blazing sunlight

are flamingos on land and flamingos in flight.

They float like swans
when the water is deep
and curl their long necks
on their backs
when they sleep.

Their chicks are downy and gray.

Darwin's Finches

They're drab in color,
small in size,
humdrum till you realize
that each of thirteen species
is explicitly unique,
distinguished from each other
by a special kind of beak.

Small beaks
from leaves and lichen pluck
insects that are out of luck.

Beaks very large and very strong
crack nutty seeds found
on the ground.

Some finches are so very cool
that they have learned
to use a tool.

Others from a cactus bloom
pick insects
that they then consume.

Still others make
delicious feasts
of ticks and flies
that bug these beasts.

Author's Note

...ed the "Islands of Enchantment," the Galápagos archipelago consists of thirteen main islands and many small ones. Early Spanish visitors found the area teeming with giant tortoises, and so they named the islands after the Spanish word for tortoises, "galápagos."

Giant tortoises can live for a year without food or water, and their meat is very good to eat, so pirates and sailors and sealers and whalers took them on board their ships. They took so many of them, in fact, that these magnificent creatures came very close to disappearing from the earth forever. Now they are carefully protected, and their numbers are increasing.

It is not just giant tortoises that are protected on the Galápagos Islands. No one is permitted to touch any of the animals, so they are not afraid of people. Perhaps that is why this blue-footed booby allowed me to take its picture. I like this photograph so much that I carry it around in my wallet with pictures of my husband and my two sons.

Contents

EQUATOR